A NOTE TO PARENTS

Congratulations on choosing the best in educational materials for your child. By selecting top-quality School Specialty products, you can be assured that the concepts used in our books will reinforce and enhance the skills that are being taught in classrooms nationwide.

And what better way to get young readers excited than with Mercer Mayer's Little Critter, a character loved by children everywhere? Our First Readers offer simple and engaging stories about Little Critter that children can read on their own. Each level incorporates reading skills, colorful illustrations, and challenging activities.

Level 1 – The stories are simple and use repetitive language. Illustrations are highly supportive.

Level 2 - The stories begin to grow in complexity. Language is still repetitive, but it is mixed with more challenging vocabulary.

Level 3 - The stories are more complex. Sentences are longer and more varied.

To help your child make the most of this book, look at the first few pictures in the story and discuss what is happening. Ask your child to predict where the story is going. Then, once your child has read the story, have him or her review the word list and do the activities. This will reinforce vocabulary words from the story and build reading comprehension.

You are your child's first and most influential teacher. No one knows your child the way you do. Tailor your time together to reinforce a newly acquired skill or to overcome a temporary stumbling block. Praise your child's progress and ideas, take delight in his or her imagination, and most of all, enjoy your time together!

This product has been aligned to state and national organization standards using the Align to Achieve Standards Database. Align to Achieve, Inc., is an indepedent, not-for-profit organization that facilitates the evaluation and improvement of academic standards and student achievement. To find how this product aligns to your standards, go to www.ChildrensSpecialty.com.

 School Specialty
Children's Publishing

Text Copyright © 2003 by School Specialty Children's Publishing, a member of the School Specialty Family.
Art Copyright © 2003 Mercer Mayer.

Send all inquiries to:
School Specialty Children's Publishing
8720 Orion Place
Columbus, OH 43240-2111

Printed in the United States of America.

1-57768-834-1

 A Big Tuna Trading Company, LLC/J. R. Sansevere Book

Library of Congress Cataloging-in-Publication Data is on file with the publisher.

4 5 6 7 8 9 10 PHXBK 09 08 07 06 05 04

FIRST READERS

Level **3**   Grades **1–2**

GOODNIGHT, LITTLE CRITTER®

by Mercer Mayer

School Specialty
Children's Publishing

Columbus, Ohio

One night, Little Sister woke me up.
She sat on my bed.
"I'm not sleepy," she said.
I knew just what to do.

GRAM

PICKLES

PEAN
BUTTE

6

"A snack will make you sleepy," I said.
We went down to the kitchen.
I made two peanut butter
and pickle sandwiches,
one for me and one for Little Sister.
Then we had a glass of milk.
"I'm still not sleepy," said Little Sister.

"Let's play a game," I said.
"A game will make you sleepy."
I got out the checkers.
I let Little Sister be red,
and I even let her win.
"Time for bed," I said.
"I'm still not sleepy," she said.

9

HUMPTY
DUMPTY

10

"A story will make you sleepy," I said.
I read Little Sister's favorite
bedtime story to her.
"Are you ready for bed now?" I asked.
"No! Not yet," said Little Sister.

11

"Maybe your teddy bear is
   getting lonely," I said.
   We went to Little Sister's room.
   Her teddy bear was in bed.
"Why don't you stay and
   keep him company," I said.
"I will, if you stay and
   keep me company," she said.
   I did not have to stay very long.

13

I went back to my own room.
I listened to the crickets.
I stared at the ceiling.
I turned one way.
I turned the other way.
Now I couldn't get to sleep.

I went to Mom and Dad's room.
I woke them up.
I sat on their bed.
"I'm not sleepy," I said.
Mom looked at Dad.
Dad looked at Mom.

They knew just what to do.

Word List

Read each word in the lists below. Then, find it in the story. Now, make up a new sentence using the word. Say your sentence out loud.

Words I Know
sleepy
said
kitchen
bedtime

Challenge Words
knew
checkers
favorite
lonely
company
crickets
ceiling

Homophones

Homophones are words that sound the same even though they mean different things and have different spellings.

Example: to, too, and two are homophones.

The words below are from the story. Try to think of a homophone for each word. Use the pictures as hints. Write your answer on a separate sheet of paper.

 **one**

for

 **no**

read

Word Scramble

Unscramble the letters below to answer the questions from the story. Write your answers on a separate sheet of paper.

What did Little Critter try first to help Little Sister fall asleep?

a kscna

What game did Little Critter and Little Sister play?

cerseckh

What did Little Critter try next?

a tsyro

What did Little Sister keep company because it was lonely?

ydted reba

Logical Reasoning

Read the clues below to figure out which book
Little Critter reads to Little Sister.

Clues
The book has a picture on the cover.
The book has words on the cover.
The title of the book is three words long.

Soft C

When the letter c is followed by an e, i, or y, it can sound like an s. This is called a soft-c sour

Example: ceiling, Maurice

Each word in the list below has a soft-c sound. Point to the two letters in each word that make that sound.

circus

cent

lace

ice

city

pencil

Pronouns

Pronouns are words that take the place of nouns. They include I, he, she, it, they, you, we, me, him, her, them, and us.

Point to the pronoun that matches the picture.

it

she

they

he

Answer Key

page 19
Homophones

won

four

know

red

page 20
Word Scramble

a snack

checkers

a story

teddy bear

page 21
Logical Reasoning

The Fuzzy Bear is Little Sister's favorite book.

page 22
Soft C

c i r c u s

c e n t

l a c e

i c e

c i t y

p e n c i l

page 23
Pronouns

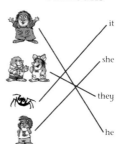

it

she

they

he